A Tale from Turkey

The Hungry Coat

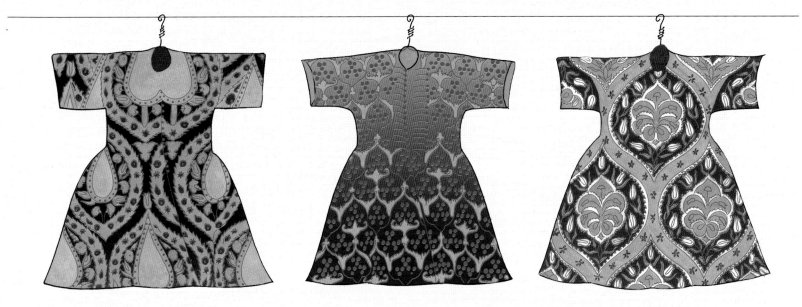

Demi

MARGARET K. McELDERRY BOOKS

NEW YORK LONDON TORONTO SYDNEY

Margaret K. McElderry Books
An imprint of Simon & Schuster Children's Publishing Division
1230 Avenue of the Americas, New York, New York 10020

Book design by Michael Nelson
The text for this book is set in Venetian 301 Demi.
The illustrations are rendered in paint and ink.
Title calligraphy by Jeanyee Wong

Manufactured in China
2 4 6 8 10 9 7 5 3

LIBRARY OF CONGRESS CATALOGING-IN-PUBLICATION DATA
Demi.
The hungry coat : a tale from Turkey / Demi.
p. cm.
Summary: After being forced to change to a fancy new coat to attend a party, Nasrettin Hoca tries to
feed his dinner to the coat, reasoning that it was the coat that was the invited guest.
ISBN 0-689-84680-0
[1. Folklore—Turkey. 2. Nasreddin Hoca (Legendary character)] I. Title.
PZ8.1.D38Hu 2004
398.2'09561'02—dc21
2002155129

For all who wear heaven
in their hearts

Once upon a time in Turkey there lived a funny, little wise man named Nasrettin Hoca. He wore a huge, white turban and a worn-out coat made of patches upon patches. Riding about on his little gray donkey, he liked to help whomever he could.

One day Nasrettin Hoca heard a great commotion inside a caravansary, a hostel for travelers. A frisky goat had gotten loose inside the kitchen. Kicking and prancing, she was breaking all the dishes, knocking over pots and pans, and spilling all the cooking oil. The cook was screaming, and a few travelers were slipping in the oil as they tried to catch the goat.

Because he loved goats so much, Nasrettin always carried a sweet apple in his pocket for them. He quickly took out the apple and cut it into little pieces. He lined up the pieces, so as the little goat nibbled to the last piece, Nasrettin was able to catch her.

Gently Nasrettin put the little goat back into her pen, and everyone cheered. The caravansary owner invited Nasrettin to eat with the other travelers, but Nasrettin declined, as he was on his way to a banquet at the home of a rich friend.

Nasrettin trotted off, waving to all and happy to have helped. He was so late now that he realized he would not have time to change his coat, which was not only worn-out with patches upon patches but also oily, dirty, and smelling of goat.

When Nasrettin's friend opened the door to Nasrettin, he was shocked. He was afraid his other guests would laugh at him for being friends with such a shabby, smelly man.

Nasrettin simply jumped off his donkey, hugged his friend, and joined the banquet. He was so happy to be among friends that for a while he didn't notice something very strange: No one was facing him!

All the guests had turned their backs toward Nasrettin. And when the servants brought dinner into the room, the food was served to everyone but him!

Before long, Nasrettin
was left sitting alone with
nothing at all to eat.
Several times he tried to
start a conversation by
yelling to a guest at the
opposite side of the room,
but no one listened and
no one responded.

Nasrettin looked thoughtfully at his friends. Each man was scrubbed until he glistened. Each one was wearing his best coat. Then Nasrettin looked down at his own coat—worn-out with patches upon patches, oily, dirty, and smelling of goat.

Very quietly Nasrettin
slipped out the door. He
mounted his little donkey
and began trotting home,
when he had an idea.

At home Nasrettin jumped into a tub of hot water, poured in a whole jar of perfumed soap crystals, and scrubbed himself until he glistened and the whole room was filled with bubbles.

Nasrettin dried and powdered himself. Then he put on new shoes with tassled toes, a magnificent new turban with sparkling jewels, and a fine new coat of shining silk with golden threads.

Nasrettin preened himself before a mirror. Never had he been so completely well dressed. Never had anyone worn a coat like this one. How fine he looked!

Nasrettin strutted out of his house. Everyone nodded respectfully as he swaggered along the street, heading back to his rich friend's home.

A servant ushered Nasrettin into the banquet hall, and his smiling host immediately served him food and drink. Everyone smiled and nodded at Nasrettin. What a fine figure he made! What a fine coat! Nasrettin was the most popular man at the banquet!

Nasrettin picked up the choicest grilled lamb chop. But instead of putting it in his mouth, Nasrettin put it inside his coat!

"Eat, coat! Eat!" said Nasrettin.

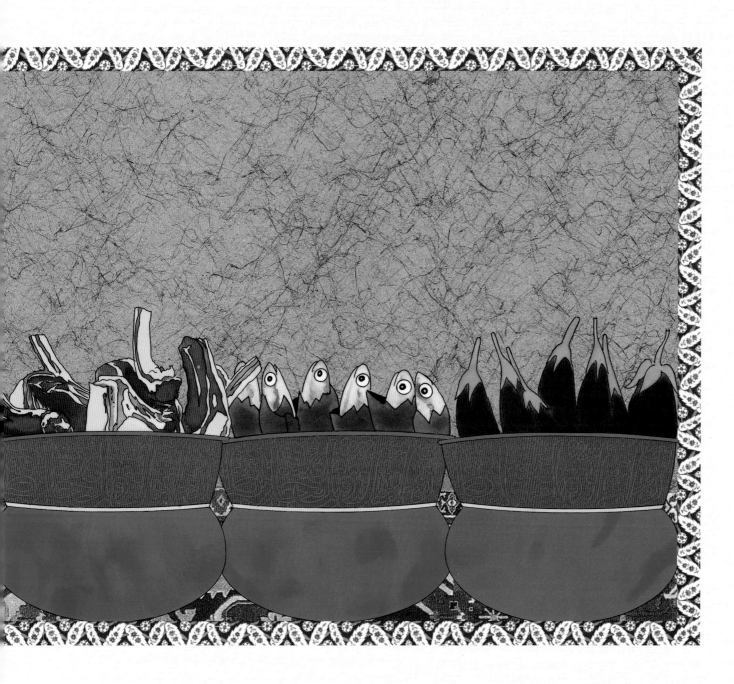

Nasrettin picked up fish fried in vine leaves and roasted eggplant. Opening his coat, he said, "Eat, coat! Eat!"

Nasrettin scooped up pilaf, raisins, and pistachio nuts. Opening his coat, he said, "Eat, coat! Eat!"

Boiled squash stuffed with hash and olives went into the coat. "Eat, coat! Eat!"

Slices of chicken breast stewed in rose water, sugar cakes, flavored jellies, sherbet, sticky baklava, pomegranates, persimmons, oranges, apples, figs, and dates—all of this food Nasrettin stuffed into his bulging coat, shouting, "Eat, coat! Eat!"

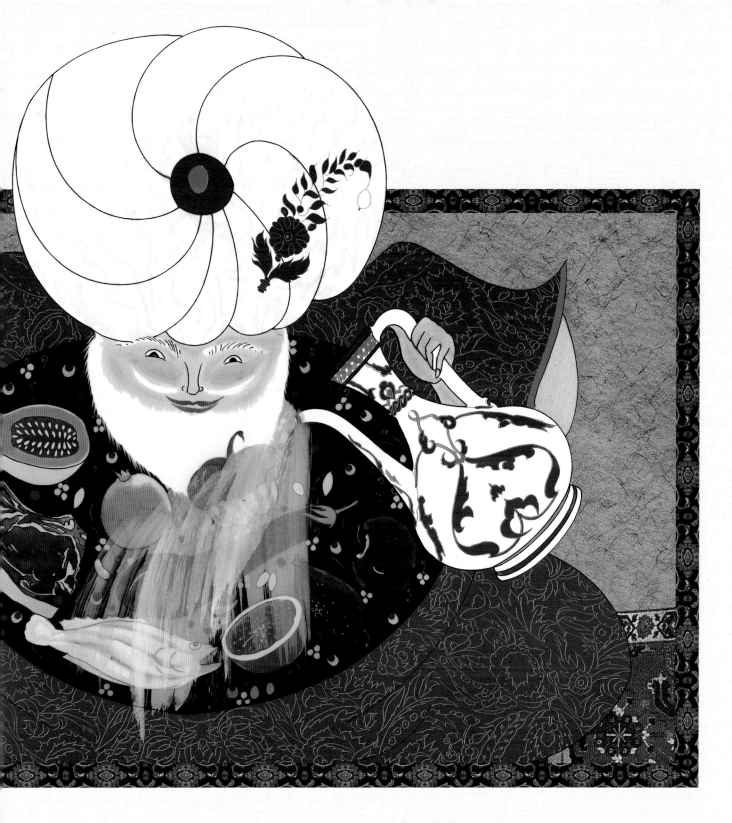

Finally Nasrettin opened his coat once more and poured a whole bottle of wine inside. Then, closing his coat as best as he could, Nasrettin patted his belly and smiled at his host.

All the guests were amazed! What was Nasrettin doing?

At last, the alarmed host said, "Tell me, my old friend, why are you feeding your coat?"

"Surely you wanted my coat to eat," Nasrettin replied. "When I first arrived in my old coat made of patches upon patches, there was no food for me. Yet when I came back in this new coat, there was every kind of food for me. This shows it was the coat—and not me—that you invited to your banquet!"

"Remember this, my friends," said Nasrettin Hoca. "If you want to look deeply, look at the man and not at his coat. You can change the coat, but you cannot change the man. A coat may be fine, but a coat does not make a man. Outside a man may wear a sheepskin, but inside he may wear the heart of a wolf! Many a good man may be found under a shabby coat. With coats, new are the best. But with friends, old are the best!"

Everyone cheered.
"The wisdom of Nasrettin Hoca calls for celebration!" exclaimed the host. Music and fireworks resounded, and everyone danced under the stars of heaven.

He who wears heaven in his heart is always well dressed.

AFTERWORD

NASRETTIN HOCA (A.D. 1208–1284) was a leading folk philosopher and humorist, born in the rural Turkish village of Hortu. His father was the imam (religious leader) of the village, and Nasrettin himself served as imam of the village before moving to the town of Akcehir to study as a dervish (master Muslim mystic) with two famous Islamic mystics.

Nasrettin became known for his common sense and droll sense of humor. He was called Hoca (or Hodja), which means "teacher" in Turkish, and stories about his adventures and wisdom became true folktales, told and embellished by adults and children alike for over seven hundred years. Today his stories are translated into many languages and are told from eastern Turkmenistan to Hungary and from southern Siberia to northern Africa, and now, in America.

With their universal themes of societal roles, survival, the joys and sorrows of daily life, and the relationships between people, people and objects, and people and animals, the stories all center around Nasrettin Hoca himself as a symbol of common sense, clear wisdom, and good-natured humor. As does *The Hungry Coat,* many of the Nasrettin Hoca stories end with a moral or clever epigram meant to teach the listener or reader a valuable life lesson.

The Nasrettin Hoca stories are immortal, as is true of all great folk art. Every year, between July 5 and July 10, the International Nasrettin Hodja Festival is held in Akcehir, where Nasrettin died and his tomb now stands. Keeping the character of Nasrettin Hoca alive through stories such as *The Hungry Coat,* writers, artists, and musicians attend the festival to create new plays, music, movies, cartoons, comic strips, and paintings about this beloved folk figure.

Maybe *you* can think up a Nasrettin Hoca story too!